Thanks, Mom and Dad, for always believing—Love, Debbie
With love to Mom, Dad, and Leslie—Susan
And to Heidi . . . the best editor to have—D & S

To Peggy
—M.G.

Text copyright © 2005 by Debbie Bertram and Susan Bloom.
Illustrations copyright © 2005 by Michael Garland.
All rights reserved under International and Pan-American Copyright Conventions.
Published in the United States by Random House Children's Books, a division of Random House, Inc., New York,
and simultaneously in Canada by Random House of Canada Limited, Toronto.

www.randomhouse.com/kids

Library of Congress Cataloging-in-Publication Data
Bertram, Debbie.
The best time to read / by Debbie Bertram and Susan Bloom ; illustrated by Michael Garland.
p.   cm.
SUMMARY: A boy who has just learned to read tries to find someone in his family who will listen to him read aloud.
ISBN 0-375-83025-1 (trade) — ISBN 0-375-93025-6 (lib. bdg.)
[1. Reading—Fiction.   2. Stories in rhyme.]   I. Bloom, Susan (Susan Lynn)
II. Garland, Michael, ill.   III. Title.

PZ8.3.B4595Bi   2005   [E]—dc22   2003026486

PRINTED IN THE UNITED STATES OF AMERICA   First Edition
10 9 8 7 6 5 4 3
RANDOM HOUSE and colophon are registered trademarks of Random House, Inc.

The Best Time to Read

by Debbie Bertram & Susan Bloom   illustrated by Michael Garland

Random House 🏠 New York

I used to read pictures,
But now I read words.
I like to read stories out loud.
I can read by myself—every book on my shelf!
It makes me feel happy and proud.

I run to the kitchen,
Where Mommy is cooking.
I ask her, "May I read to you?"

She tells me, "You bet! But I don't have time yet.
Right now I am making beef stew."

I look for my daddy—
He's in the backyard.
"Daddy, Daddy! May I read to you?"

"I do love your reading, but I'm mowing and weeding.
I'll have time as soon as I'm through."

A sign says, KEEP OUT!
On my big brother's door.
He's at his computer all day.
Instant messages chime—and he *never* has time!
"I'm busy," he says. "Go away."

In my big sister's room
There are clothes *everywhere*.
I open my book. "Want to see?"

"I have friends stopping by. Maybe later, I'll try.
Do you like this new sweater on me?"

Baby *loves* to hear stories—
So I tiptoe in . . . *shhhh*.
I'll read for a nap-time surprise.
She gurgles and slurps, drinks her bottle and burps.
She yawns and then closes her eyes.

I march into the den.
"Hi, Grandma. Hi, Grandpa.
Look at my book and what's in it!"

My grandma says, "Great! But you'll just have to wait.
The news will be done in a minute."

"Is a minute done yet?"
I look up at the clock.
I *tap, tap* my foot on the floor.
While Grandma is sitting and doing her knitting,
My grandpa is starting to snore!

I can read to the dog!
"Here, Rover! Come listen.
My story is really a winner."
I start reading to Rover, but quickly that's over.
Plink, plunk! He hears kibble—his dinner!

No one has time
To listen to me.
Guess I'll go to my bedroom upstairs.
But waiting for me . . . is my *toy* family.
I can read to my bunnies and bears!

I am reading out loud,
When I hear . . . *knock, knock, knock.*
And guess who is there at the door?
"We've been waiting," they tease.
"Will you read to us, please?"
Rover follows and flops on the floor.

"You're all here! Come on in!"
I turn back to page one.
It's 100 percent guaranteed . . .
That it's more fun to share with your family there.
Right NOW is the best time to read!